THE RIDDLE
OF THE
RED PURSE

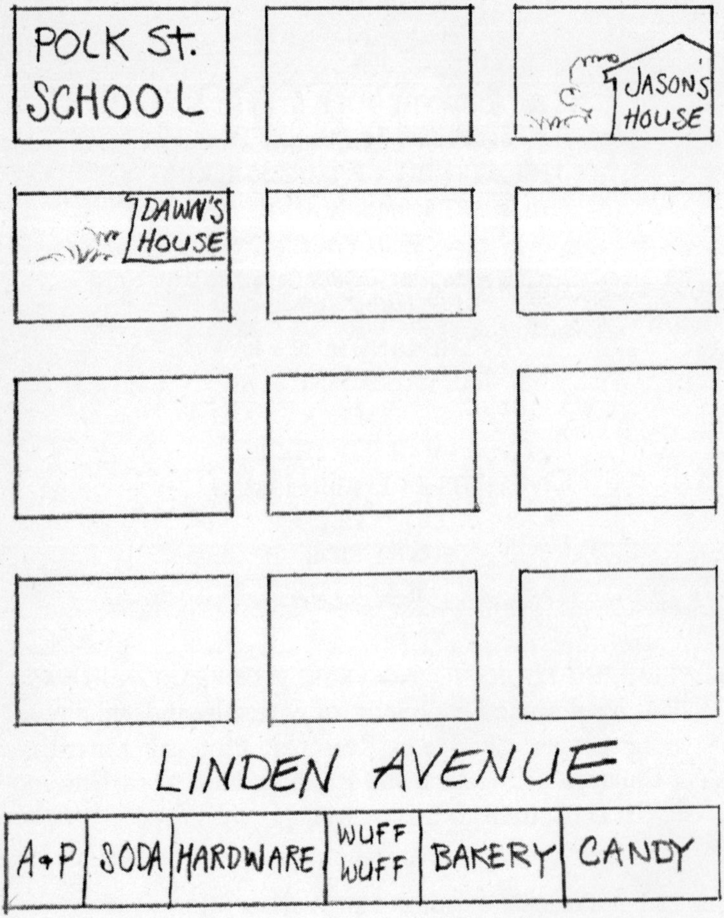
POLK ST. SCHOOL
JASON'S HOUSE
DAWN'S HOUSE
LINDEN AVENUE
A+P
SODA
HARDWARE
WUFF WUFF
BAKERY
CANDY

THE RIDDLE
OF THE
RED PURSE

Patricia Reilly Giff

Illustrated by Blanche Sims

A YOUNG YEARLING BOOK

Published by
Dell Publishing Co., Inc.
1 Dag Hammarskjold Plaza
New York, New York 10017

Yearling ® TM 913705, Dell Publishing Co., Inc.

ISBN: 0-440-47534-1

Printed in the United States of America

October 1987

10 9 8 7 6 5 4 3 2 1

W

Love and welcome
to
Jeanne Patricia Lyons
born August 9, 1986

THE RIDDLE
OF THE
RED PURSE

··· CHAPTER 1 ···

Ms. Rooney was writing on the board.

Dawn Bosco crossed her fingers.

She saw Linda Lorca cross hers too.

"Paper monitor," Ms. Rooney wrote. "Sherri Dent."

Good. Dawn didn't want to be paper monitor.

"Erase boards," Ms. Rooney wrote. "Jason Bazyk."

Dawn crossed her fingers harder.

She was dying to be class president.

She bet Linda Lorca was too.

"Fish monitor: Jill Simon."

Dawn sat back. Who cared about being fish monitor?

"I have fish at home," Jill said. "Two guppies. One swordtail. Three—"

Jill was always talking about her birthday fish.

She had even brought fish food for show-and-tell.

Yucks.

Ms. Rooney began to write again: "Class president."

Dawn crossed her toes.

Class president was the best job.

Ms. Rooney wrote a big *D*.

"Dawn Bosco, I bet," said Linda Lorca. "That bossy thing."

"I am not," said Dawn.

Ms. Rooney wrote the rest of Dawn's name.

Class president! She couldn't believe it.

Linda Lorca put her tongue out.

Dawn wanted to stick hers out too.

She didn't, though.

Ms. Rooney said the president had to be good as gold.

Ms. Rooney wiped the chalk dust off her hands. "Do good jobs."

She looked at Dawn.

It was time for the pledge.

That was the president's job.

Dawn rushed to the front. "Class, stand," she said in a nice loud voice.

Half the class stood.

"Just a minute," Jill said. "I have to feed the fish."

Alex Walker stuck his head out of the closet. "Hold on," he said. "I have to find my homework."

"You should have done that before," Dawn said. She tried to sound like Ms. Rooney.

"I told you she was bossy," said Linda Lorca.

Ms. Rooney shook her head at Linda.

"I pledge allegiance," Dawn began.

The rest of the class said the pledge too.

Then it was time for show-and-tell.

Dawn had something to show.

Something important.

She looked at the box under her desk.

Could she call on herself first?

Maybe not.

Everyone was raising his hand.

Dawn made believe she didn't see Jill Simon.

Jill would show-and-tell for too long.

She wasn't going to call on Linda Lorca.

She called on Sherri Dent.

Sherri went to the front. "I have something to tell."

"I hope everyone is listening," Dawn said. She smiled the way Ms. Rooney did.

"Do you see I'm a little tan?" Sherri asked.

"You look good," said Jason.

"I went to California for the winter break," said Sherri. "I swam every day."

She waved her arms around. "This is me swimming."

"Go, go, go," said Jason.

Dawn looked at the back of the room.

Jill Simon was bending over the fish tank.

One of her braids was getting wet.

Dawn frowned.

Jill should be paying attention.

Sherri went back to her seat.

"Now I have something to show," Dawn said.

She pulled a polka dot box up to the front.

She opened it for the class.

"Wow," said Sherri.

On top was a pink polka dot hat.

Dawn put it on her head.

"This box helps me solve mysteries," she said. "It has all the detective stuff."

"Dawn thinks she knows everything," Linda Lorca said.

"I found Emily's ring last time," Dawn said. "The blue one. Didn't I?"

"That's right," said Emily.

"Your hat is a little big," Sherri said.

"Miles too big," said Linda Lorca. "Elephant head."

Dawn made a face at Linda. She held up a magnifying glass. "I have a wig too. No-one can tell who I am."

"Neat," said Sherri.

"Yes," said Ms. Rooney. She came to the front of the room. "It's time for math now."

Dawn pushed the box back to her desk.
She sniffed when she passed Linda Lorca.
She was sick of being good as gold.
If only she could find a mystery.
She'd solve it right this minute.
Linda Lorca would be sorry.
That big baby.

···CHAPTER 2···

It was after school.

Dawn stood near the schoolyard fence.

She closed her eyes tight.

A snowflake landed on her nose.

"No peeking," Jason shouted.

Dawn listened hard. Jason was running around the side of the school.

She could hear him.

She could always hear Jason. He was loud.

"Ten. Twenty. Thirty. Here I come," Dawn yelled. "Ready or not."

She opened her eyes.

The ground was white.

So were the tops of the swings.

The sky was dark, though. It was almost time to go home.

Dawn looked around.

Jason's footprints were gone.

She ran toward the school.

The wind blew hard. It pulled at her scarf.

It was a great scarf.

The best in the class.

Noni had made it for her.

Dawn ran around the side of the school.

Jason was gone.

She waited. She listened.

It was hard to hear in the snow and the wind.

She had to hear him.

She had to find him.

They were playing detective.

Jason was a thief. He had taken a million dollars.

She was the detective.

Jason should be easy to catch. She had caught him before.

She'd put him in jail again.

Jail was under the picnic table.

She took a few steps.

It was really dark in back of the school.

She turned around. Everyone else had gone.

She took one more step.

Her heart thumped.

What if a real thief were there?

What if he jumped out at her?

What if . . .

She took a step backward.

She heard something.

Someone was behind her.

Maybe a killer.

Before she could turn, something grabbed her.

"Yeow," she yelled. "Noni."

"Some detective you are," Jason said. "Have to call your grandmother."

"I was not," Dawn said. "I was singing."

She opened her mouth. "No-ni-la-la," she sang.

She liked the way it sounded.

Noni always told her to sing. "Bellissimo," she'd say.

That meant "gorgeous."

Dawn sang a little louder.

Jason put his hands over his ears. "Yeow," he said.

Jim came over.

He was the man who cleaned the school.

"Playing hide-and-seek?"

"Sort of," Dawn said.

"It's getting dark," said Jim.

"My turn," Jason said.

"No one's turn," said Jim. "I have to close the gates."

Dawn dusted the snow off her scarf.

They started for the gate.

Then she remembered.

"My mittens."

"What about them?" Jason asked.

"I left them on the swing. Remember? They were soaking wet."

Jason looked back. "It's too late to get them."

Dawn put her lip out. "It is not. They have hearts on the fingers. They have flowers on the backs. Noni made them."

Dawn ran fast. She sang, "Ni-la-la-ni."

What if Jim closed the gates?

It would be cold in the schoolyard tonight.
Freezing.

She was hungry too. Her mother was making Friday-night meatballs.

She ran fast.

She scooped up her mittens.

They were a mess. It looked as if the hearts were melting.

Then she saw something. Something red and shiny.

It was somebody's purse.

"Hurry," Jason yelled.

She thought about Jim closing the gates.

She grabbed the purse.

She put it in her pocket. She started to run.

···CHAPTER 3···

It was Sunday afternoon.

Dawn took her last bite of cake.

Then she slapped her head.

"What's the matter?" her mother asked.

"Dawn's slapping a bug," her brother Chris said.

"There aren't any bugs in the winter," said Dawn.

Chris started to laugh. He pointed at her. "You're the bug."

Dawn crossed her eyes at him. Then she looked at her mother. "I just remembered something. I have to go to Jason's."

She ran up to her room.

She put on her coat and her polka dot hat.

The hat fell down over her eyes.

Dawn took a sock.

She put it in the hat.

Just right. She could see.

She dragged her detective box downstairs.

Noni was watching basketball on TV.

She smiled at Dawn.

Noni went to the closet. She brought back her grey scarf.

"What is that for?" Dawn asked.

"It's freezing out," Noni said.

Noni put the scarf around Dawn's head. She kissed her cheeks. "You'll be nice and warm."

Dawn went outside.

She hoped no one would see the scarf.

It made her look like a hippopotamus. A fat grey one.

It kept her polka dot hat on tight, though.

She began to sing. "Frosty the la-la. Had a very la-la nose."

She wished she knew the words.

Across the street she saw Chris and his friend Donny.

They were looking for something.

"Is that your sister?" Donny asked. "The one with the thing on her head?"

"That crazy-looking kid?" Chris said. "Don't be silly."

Dawn put her hands on her hips. "I am so, Christopher Bosco."

Chris started to make a snowball.

Dawn pulled her box around the corner. She went as fast as she could.

Jason was outside his house. He was making a snowman.

It had stone ears and a rock nose.

"Give me your scarf," he told Dawn.

"We can't play snowman," she said. "We have a mystery."

"Yahoo," Jason said. He rubbed his mittens together.

"Why are you wearing one red mitten and one green one?" she asked.

"Simple," Jason said. "I lost one red one and one green one."

"Look what I found." Dawn took the red purse out of her pocket.

They went into Jason's house.

Jason had a terrible playroom.

It had an ironing board in the middle.

It had a TV, a black-and-white one.

It had two old orange chairs.

Jason sat in one.

Dawn sat in the other.

"Open it up," Jason said.

"Wait till you see," said Dawn.

She snapped open the purse.

Jason bent over to look.

He fell off the orange chair.

"There's a paper with writing," Dawn told him. "And money too."

She scooped everything out.

There was gritty stuff on the bottom. Sand or something.

It got under her fingernails.

"Yucks," she said.

Jason held up the paper. "It's a list for the stores."

A&P	WUFF WUFF'S PET STORE
MILK	FOOD FOR ANGEL
BRED	
CHEESE	

"Double yucks," Dawn said. "I hate cheese."

"Look at the money," Jason said.

Dawn put the money on the ironing board. One dime. One nickel. Two pennies.

"Sixteen cents," she said.

Jason rolled the dime across the board. "Seventeen."

He looked at her. "We could buy Gummy Bears."

Dawn shook her head. "We're detectives."

Jason's mother came to the door.

"We have a mystery to solve," Jason told her.

"I hope it's the mystery of the missing mittens," she said. "How about some cookies?"

"Great," Dawn said. She hoped they were chocolate chips.

Jason took the magnifying glass out of the box.

He looked at the gritty stuff in the purse.

"Looks like crackers," he said. "The vanilla kind."

Mrs. Bazyk came back with the cookies.

They were the fig kind.

They had things that got caught in your teeth.

Dawn shivered.

Jason put two in his mouth. "It's the riddle of the red purse," he said. Cookie crumbs flew all over.

"What's a riddle?" Dawn asked.

"It's like a mystery." He looked up. "What can we do?"

Dawn took a cookie.

She was starving to death.

"I have an idea," she said.

···CHAPTER 4···

Ms. Rooney called the roll.

Today three people were out. Sherri, Linda, and Jill.

Dawn had a little cold too.

Noni had given her cough drops.

The brown kind.

Dawn put them in the back of her desk.

Then she went up to Ms. Rooney. "Can Jason and I put up some signs?"

"May I," Ms. Rooney said. She looked at the signs.

POLKA DOT PRIVATE EYE
FOUND
RED PURSE
17 cents
See Dawn. See Jason.
Room 113.

"Nice," said Ms. Rooney. "Go ahead."
Dawn put one in the front of the room.
Then they went out to the hall.
Jason stuck a sign on the bulletin board.
Dawn put one on the art teacher's door.
They put one in the gym.
"Now what?" Jason asked.
"Now nothing," Dawn said. "We have to
go back. We have to do math and stuff."
"Yucks," said Jason.
"Double yucks," said Dawn.
She tried to think.
What else could they do?

"Wait a minute," said Jason. "I thought of something."

Too bad, Dawn thought.

She was the real detective.

She should have thought of something.

"We could ask the principal," Jason said. "We could talk on the speaker."

"Right," said Dawn. "Tell the whole school."

They rushed down the hall.

"Why not?" said Mr. Mancina. He turned on the switch.

Dawn said, "A-hem." She tried to make her voice sound important. "This is the Polka Dot Private Eye."

Jason leaned over. He almost knocked the speaker off the table. "It's Jason too," he said.

"We found a purse," said Dawn. "It has seventeen cents." She wished Jason didn't take up so much room.

"Come to Room One-thirteen," said Jason.

Mr. Mancina patted them on their shoulders. "Good thinking."

They started back for the classroom.

They stopped for a drink.

Then they looked out the door. It was snowing.

"I forgot," Dawn said. "I'm the class president."

"So?"

"We have to go right back. I have to be good as gold."

They hurried back to the classroom.

"We heard you," said Richard Best.

"Lucky," said Emily Arrow. "I always wanted to talk on that thing."

Ms. Rooney clapped her hands. "It's time to start spelling," she said. "Take out a piece of paper."

Just then the door opened.

It was Holly Best, Richard's sister.

"You found my purse," she said.

Ms. Rooney looked up.

The door opened again.

It was Chris's friend Donny. "I've been looking all over. Where's the purse?"

"A boy doesn't have a purse," said Dawn.

"It's my sister's," Donny said. "She's going to kill me if I don't give it back."

"Hey," said Holly Best. "That purse is mine. Seventeen cents and everything."

Dawn looked at Jason.

Ms. Rooney frowned. "Settle this after school."

"I'll be on the school steps," said Donny. "At three o'clock."

Holly made a face. "Don't worry. I'll be there too."

They went out the door.

Dawn took out a piece of paper.
She put her name on it.
She tried to think.
Now they really had a riddle!

···CHAPTER 5···

Dawn was ready to cry.

Emily had a hundred percent on her spelling.

So did Jason.

Dawn had two wrong. Only ninety percent.

Ms. Rooney was giving out stars. Green ones.

She went around the room. "Good work," she told Emily.

"Terrific," she said to Jason.

She looked at Dawn's paper. "Try to learn those words. Write them three times."

Dawn looked down.

She had spelled *careful* wrong. C-a-r-ef-u-l-l.

She leaned over.

Emily had spelled *careful* with one *l*.

Dawn clicked her teeth.

She looked at her paper again.

Bread was spelled wrong too.

She had forgotten the *e*.

Bread.

It made her think of something.

What?

She couldn't remember.

"Put your papers away," Ms. Rooney said. "It's time for gym."

The class went down the hall.

Jason walked with Dawn. "What do you think?" he asked. "Is the purse Holly's or Donny's?"

"That's what we have to find out," Dawn said.

Mr. Bell came to the gym door. "Today we're going to have relay races."

Dawn kept thinking about the purse.

She thought during gym.

She thought at recess.

That afternoon they had handwriting.

Dawn was a good writer.

She made tall, straight I's.

She made big, loopy B's.

Then her mouth opened.

She remembered something.

At last it was three o'clock. She walked down the hall with Jason.

"What are we going to do?" Jason asked.

"Don't worry," Dawn said.

They opened the big brown doors.

Donny wasn't there yet.

Holly jumped off the steps. "Where's my purse?"

Dawn took a breath.

She was glad she had thought all day. "I have to ask you a question," she told Holly.

"Right," said Jason.

Dawn sat down on the step. She pulled out her polka dot hat.

"Silly," said Holly.

Dawn put on the hat. She could feel the steps were wet from the snow.

She stood up quickly.

"What question?" Holly asked.

"How do you spell *Bread*?" Dawn asked.

"I think you're crazy," Holly said. "You're as crazy as my brother Richard."

Jason jumped up on the step. "Spell it."

Holly looked up at the sky. "Bread," she said. "B-r-e-a-d."

"Too bad," Dawn said.

"Too bad," said Jason. He looked at Dawn. "Why?"

"You'd better keep looking for your purse," said Dawn. "This one isn't yours."

"You think you know everything," Holly said. "Even that dumb Linda Lorca said so yesterday."

Holly sat down on the steps.

Dawn opened her mouth.

Then she closed it again.

Let Holly get a wet seat.

It served her right.

Dawn pulled out the purse. She showed them the store list.

"Look," she said.

MILK

BRED

CHEESE

"I hate cheese," Holly said.

Dawn pointed. "The person doesn't know how to spell *bread*."

Holly looked at the purse. "Hey," she said. "That's not mine. Mine was bigger. Fatter."

Holly stood up.

The back of her was wet. "Squish," she said. She raced down the street.

Just then Donny opened the school door.

"Let me," said Jason. "Hey, Donny. Spell *bread*."

"Out of my way," Donny said. "I'm going to miss the bus."

"What about the purse?" Dawn called after him.

He waved a purse in the air.
It was more orange than red.
"Found it," he yelled. "Thanks."
Dawn looked at Jason.
He had peanut butter all over his mouth.
"We have to start over again," she said.
He wiped it off. "Good."

···CHAPTER 6···

Dawn was late for school. Very late.

Her mother had made her go back upstairs. She had to wear an undershirt.

It was tan. The yuck kind.

She was wearing a brand-new sweater, though. Pink and purple. It was gorgeous.

Noni had made it for her.

Dawn was the last one in the classroom.

Everyone was hanging up his coat and hat.

Ms. Rooney looked up. She smiled at Dawn. "Good," she said. "Everyone is here today."

Dawn went to her seat.

It was hard not to yawn.

She had stayed awake late last night.

She had been reading *The Polka Dot Private Eye Book*.

It was great.

It told her how to solve mysteries.

Linda and Sherri and Jill were in back.

They were fighting.

It was a whisper fight.

They didn't want Ms. Rooney to hear.

Ms. Rooney didn't like fighting.

Linda saw Dawn. "It's all your fault," she said.

Jill was crying. "I want my purse."

"You mean, my purse," said Sherri.

"No, mine," said Linda.

Dawn pulled off her jacket.

She saw Linda look at her sweater.

Good thing she didn't know about the undershirt.

Dawn thought about her book. It said:

ASK QUESTIONS.

YOU'LL FIND THINGS OUT.

She looked at Jill. "What does your purse look like?"

"Red," said Jill.

"Mine too," said Sherri.

Linda put her nose up close to Dawn. "Red," she said in a loud voice. She looked up at Ms. Rooney.

Ms. Rooney was writing in her book.

She wasn't watching.

"I know red," said Dawn. She talked as loud as Linda. "But how big? How fat? Stuff like that."

"They're all the same," said Jill.

"They can't be," Dawn said.

"Smarty pants," said Linda. "We made them at Brownies."

Just then Ms. Rooney stood up. "Class President," she said, "it's time for the pledge."

Dawn raced to the front of the room.

"Class, stand," she said.

She looked at Jill.

She looked at Sherri.

She looked at Linda.

Whose purse was it?

The class said the pledge.

Then Jill had something to show. It was a picture of her new fish.

Jason had something to show too.

It was a letter from his pen pal.

He read it out loud.

He made lots of mistakes.

Jason wasn't such a good reader.

Then it was time to copy the board story.

It was a story about the sunny South.

It was easy.

Dawn raced through it.

Sherri raised her hand. "I was in California," she said. "Remember? I went swimming. That's like the sunny South."

Ms. Rooney smiled. "That's true."

Dawn tore three pages out of her notebook.

She wrote the same thing on each paper.

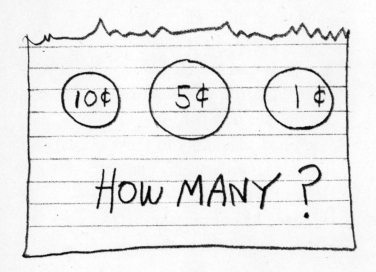

10¢   5¢   1 ¢

HOW MANY ?

Gorgeous, she thought.

She went up to the pencil sharpener.

On the way back she dropped a paper on Jill's desk.

She put one on Sherri's.

She put one on Linda's.

Ms. Rooney looked up. "Good as gold," she reminded Dawn.

Dawn went back to her desk.

She'd have the mystery solved in no time.

··· CHAPTER 7 ···

It was time for lunch.

Ms. Rooney's class marched down to the cafeteria.

"Well?" Sherri said.

"How about it?" asked Linda.

Jill didn't say anything. She just sniffed.

Dawn raised one shoulder. "I didn't look yet. My group had reading. I had math and everything."

"Time to eat," the lunch monitor said. "You can talk later."

Dawn slid into the seat next to Jason.

Jason was having peanut butter and jelly.

That's what he always had.

Dawn had cheese.

"Want to swap?" she asked him.

"Are you kidding?" He took a big bite. The jelly dripped on the table.

Jill was at the next table. She leaned over. "I'll swap," she said. "I love cheese."

Dawn ate Jill's ham sandwich.

She started her dessert.

Apples and cookies.

The best kind.

She told Jason about the papers.

"Great idea," said Jason. "There was one dime, one nickel, and two pennies. Right?"

"Right," said Dawn. "Careful with that jelly. It'll get on my sweater."

She opened the first paper.
It was Sherri's.
It said:

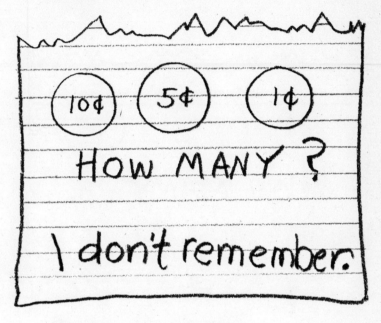

"Sherri is out," said Jason.
"I guess so," Dawn said.
Jill's paper was next.
Jason leaned over Dawn's shoulder. He smelled like peanut butter.

Dawn tried not to breathe.

She looked down. Jill's paper was a mess.

It had a tearstain on the bottom.

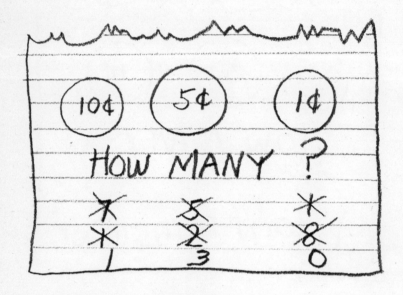

"Wrong," said Jason.

"All wrong," said Dawn.

Just then Linda came over.

She had ketchup on her mouth.

She wiped some of it off.

"Where's my purse?" she asked.
Dawn opened Linda's paper.
It said:

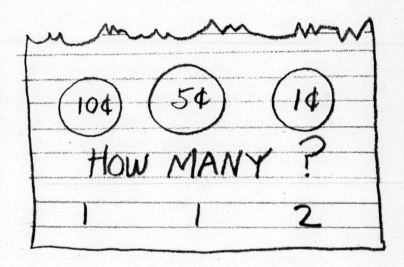

HOW MANY?

10¢	5¢	1¢
1	1	2

Jason and Dawn looked at each other.
She reached into her pocket.
The riddle was over.
She was sorry.
Jason was too, she thought.

"Here it is," she said to Linda.

"How about a reward?" Jason asked. "We could buy some Gummy Bears."

"Reward?" Linda said.

She opened the purse. "Hey. This isn't mine. This ugly thing. The stitches are all crooked."

"Not yours?" Dawn said.

"Not yours?" said Jason. "Give it back."

Linda dropped the purse on the table.

It landed on the jelly.

Dawn wiped the purse off. "Sticky," she said.

"Now what?" Jason asked.

Just then Sherri came over. "Where's my purse?"

Dawn shook her head. "Sorry," she said. "You couldn't remember the numbers."

The bell rang.

The lunch monitor blew her whistle.

"Line up," she yelled. "Time to go back to the classroom."

"Not fair," said Sherri.

"Not fair," said Jill.

Jason and Dawn went to the end of the line.

"Now what?" said Jason.

"Now we still have a riddle," said Dawn.

···CHAPTER 8···

Dawn banged open the school door.

"Hurry," she told Jason.

Jason stuck out his lip. "I'm sick of hurrying. I hurried all day long."

"Don't you watch TV?" Dawn shook her head. "Detectives hurry. They run all over the place."

Jason jumped off the steps. He threw himself onto a snow pile. "Stop, thief," he yelled.

He brushed the snow off his jeans. "Too bad we don't have a thief."

Dawn nodded. "There is something we can do."

"What?"

"We'll stop at my house first," she said. "Get some cookies."

She looked at her birthday watch.

It had a green face.

It had purple hands.

It said three-thirty.

She wished Jason would stop fooling around. He was jumping up and down in the snow.

He threw a snowball at the telephone pole.

"We can go to my house," Jason said. "My mother has some fig cookies left."

Dawn looked up at the flag pole.

The wind was blowing the flag back and forth.

She shook her head back and forth too.

They had sugar cookies at her house.

Noni had made them yesterday.

"My house is on the way," she said.

Jason shook his hands in the air. "It's freezing," he said. "On the way where?"

"On the way to Wuff Wuff's Pet Store."

"Good idea," he said. He stopped to think. "Why?"

"We can show the list to the man," Dawn said. "Maybe he'll remember someone with a red purse."

Jason blew on his fingers. "Let's hurry. We don't have all day. I have homework to do."

They raced down the street.

They stopped at Dawn's house.

Dawn threw her books onto the table.

She took two cookies.

One for her. One for Jason.

Noni smiled. "Take two more."

Jason took a bite. "Almost as good as my mother's fig cookies."

Outside they hurried around the corner.

It was a long walk to Linden Avenue. The wind was blowing hard.

Dawn kept turning in circles.

"I'm a windmill," she yelled.

At Wuff Wuff's, Dawn put her hands over her ears.

Dogs were barking.

Cats were meowing.

Birds were squawking.

A hamster raced around on a runner.

"Look at that guy go," Jason said.

Dawn nodded. "He loves it."

The man was in the back. He was dropping fish food into a tank.

"Pretty," said Dawn.

She watched the fish swimming around.

"Can I help you?" asked the man.

Dawn held out the purse. "We found this."

"It's not mine," the man said. "Ask one of the snakes."

He started to laugh. He slapped his leg.

Dawn pulled out the list.

"See," she said. " 'Food for Angel.' "

The man scratched his head. "We had kittens last week."

He looked up at the ceiling. "Yes. Someone came in and bought one. I think she called her Angel."

Dawn leaned closer.

So did Jason.

Jason smelled like sugar cookies.

"What did she look like?" Dawn asked.

"Skinny like a stick," said the man. "Red hair. Brown eyes. A skillion freckles."

Dawn raised one shoulder. "I don't know anyone with red hair."

"What's her name?" Jason asked.

"Cindy," he said. "No, Candy." He scratched his head again. "Maybe it was Catherine."

"Think hard," Jason told the man.

"Katie," said the man.

"How old was she?" Dawn asked.

"Fifteen," said the man. "Sixteen."

Dawn sighed. "Thanks anyway. It's the wrong person."

They started back out of the store.

They stopped to watch the fish again.

One of the fish was swimming along the bottom.

It swam around a little castle in the sand.

"Come on," Jason said. "We have homework."

They went outside.

"How do you know it was the wrong girl?" Jason asked.

"There are no teenagers in our school," Dawn said. "Only kids from six to twelve."

"So?" Jason asked.

"So she couldn't have dropped the purse in the schoolyard."

Jason sighed. "We walked all the way here for nothing."

Dawn shook her head.

The wind blew her scarf across her face.

"Not for nothing," she said. "I was wrong about something."

She tucked her scarf around her neck. "I think I can solve the mystery." She nodded. "Tomorrow."

···CHAPTER 9···

Today there was more snow.

Dawn wore her red boots. They came up to her knees.

She gave Noni a quick kiss. "I have to hurry."

Dawn was the first one in the school-yard.

The snow was high.

She waded through it.

She bumped into the picnic table.

She fished around underneath. Then she put something in her schoolbag.

The school bus stopped at the gate.

Other children were coming.

She saw Jason. He was hopping across the snow.

"Are you ready to solve the riddle?" he asked.

"Two of them," Dawn said.

They went inside. Jason pulled off his hat. Snow flew all over.

Dawn reached into her schoolbag.

She pulled out a mitten. A red one. "The mystery of the missing mitten," she said.

Jason's eyes opened.

"My detective book says 'THINK,'" said Dawn. "I thought. I remembered. The picnic table was our jail. You left the red mitten in jail."

"Bad news," Jason said. He held up his hand.

"What?" Dawn asked. She marched along. She liked the slap-slap her boots made.

"I lost the other red one. I lost the green one too." He raised his shoulders in the air.

They went into the classroom.

Dawn pinned her boots with a clothespin.

She went to the back of the room.

She said hello to Drake and Harry, the class fish.

Jill was feeding them.

Dawn went up to Ms. Rooney's desk.

She whispered in her ear.

Ms. Rooney kept nodding. She was smiling too.

It was time for the pledge.

Today everyone was ready.

Then it was time for show-and-tell.

"I have to call on myself first," Dawn said.

Linda Lorca clicked her teeth.

Dawn held the purse up in the air. "I've solved the riddle of the red purse," she said.

"Me too," said Jason.

Dawn opened the purse. "See this stuff in the bottom."

"It looks like vanilla cookies," Jason said.

"It looks like sand too," said Dawn.

Sherri raised her hand. "There was sand in California. Lots of it. I went swimming every day."

Dawn nodded. "At first I thought the purse was yours."

"Even though you didn't remember the dimes and the pennies and the nickels," said Jason.

Dawn walked to the back of the room.

"Look, everybody," she said.

Everyone stood up.

"I see Drake," said Sherri. "Harry too."

"Look at the fish food," said Dawn. She held up the box.

She poured a little into her hand.

She took a little of the sandy stuff out of the purse.

"It's the same," said Jason.

Dawn looked at Jill.

Jill was smiling. She was nodding her head up and down. "I put some fish food in the purse," she said. "I brought it for show-and-tell."

"Here's your purse," said Dawn.

Jill came to the back of the room.

"You're a great detective," she told Dawn. "How did you guess?"

Dawn held up her fingers. "I'll bet you bought your fish at Wuff Wuff's."

"Right," said Jill. She tucked her purse in her pocket. "My angelfish. I buy my fish food there too. The fish just love it."

Dawn took a breath. "One more thing. You're the only one who likes cheese."

Ms. Rooney smiled.

Emily Arrow clapped.

Linda raised her hand high. "Wait a minute," she said. "Jill had the pennies wrong. She had the nickels wrong. She even had the dimes wrong."

Jill looked as if she were going to cry. "I can't help it," she said. "I'm terrible at math."

Linda nodded. She looked at Dawn. "Not bad," she said. She started to smile.

Dawn smiled too.

She went back to her seat.

The riddle was solved.

She couldn't wait for the next mystery.

She hoped it would happen soon.

The Kids of the Polk Street School

Laugh with this funny class of sometimes *really good* sometimes *really mischievous* boys and girls!

by Patricia Reilly Giff

___#1	THE BEAST IN MS. ROONEY'S ROOM	40485-1	$2.25
___#2	FISH FACE	42557-3	2.25
___#3	THE CANDY CORN CONTEST	41072-X	2.25
___#4	DECEMBER SECRETS	41795-3	2.25
___#5	IN THE DINOSAUR'S PAW	44150-1	2.25
___#6	THE VALENTINE STAR	49204-1	2.25
___#7	LAZY LIONS, LUCKY LAMBS	44640-6	2.50
___#8	SNAGGLE DOODLES	48068-X	2.50
___#9	PURPLE CLIMBING DAYS	47309-8	2.50
___#10	SAY ''CHEESE''	47639-9	2.25
___#11	SUNNY SIDE UP	48406-5	2.25
___#12	PICKLE PUSS	46844-2	2.25